THE SPECTACULAR ADVENTURES OF

SOPHIE AND SEBASTIAN

WRITTEN AND ILLUSTRATED BY
RUTH JEYAVEERAN

Houghton Mifflin Company Boston 2005

Sophie was a hippo hungry for some action. Wading in the lake, she dreamed of flying through the air on a skateboard.

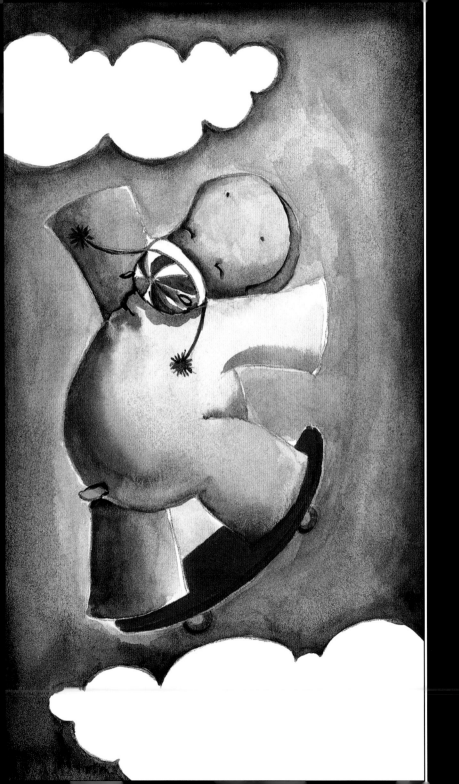

KABOOM! Sophie's dream was preposterous for a hippopotamus. Even her best friend, Sebastian, thought it might be a humongous mistake for Sophie to skate.

When she wasn't trying to skate,

Sophie baked chunky peanut butter and jelly cookies,

played the drums in a band called The Hip-Os,

and collected vintage comics.

She had nine pairs of sneakers

and made her own clothes.

But Sophie's favorite thing to do was draw. She kept a secret sketchbook, which no one except Sebastian was allowed to see.

Every afternoon Sophie drew in her secret sketchbook, stared into the sky, and fantasized about the perfect **JUMBO-SIZE** board strong enough to support her hefty proportions.

While she dreamed, the other hippos gossiped and blew bubbles. "That Sophie always has her head in the clouds," they grumbled. "Why can't she settle down to the bottom of the lake like the rest of us?"

But Sophie didn't listen to them . . .

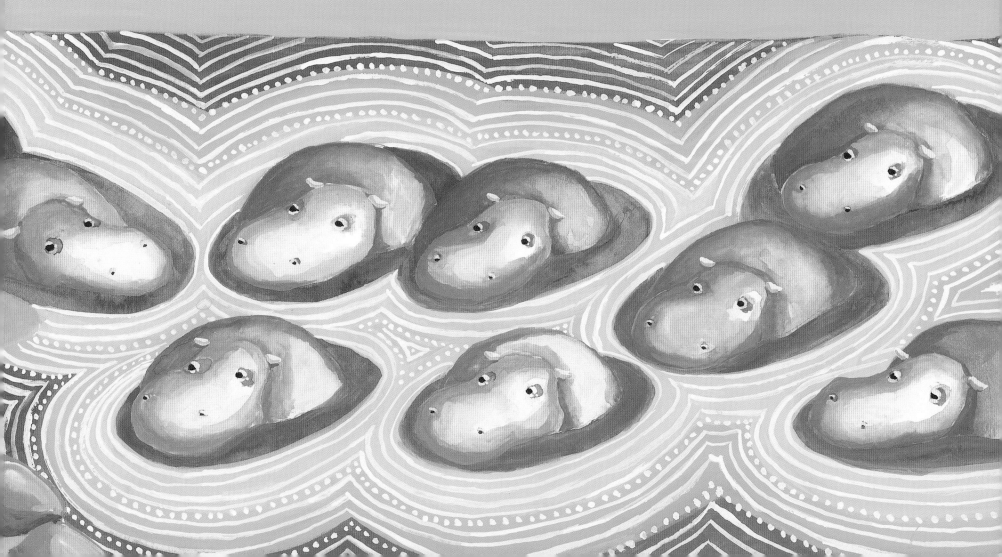

Sophie gritted her blunt teeth, stuck out her wide jaw, and said,
"I'm not giving up. I don't want to sink or swim. I want to soar!"
But without any more boards to break, Sophie was stumped.

DICTIONARY

BIRDBRAIN'S

NINTH EDITION

KRACK! She was too busy breaking bigger and bigger skateboards to care.

Finally, when she had smashed her last skateboard, Sebastian looked up from his dictionary. "Sophie, maybe it's time to give up your dream and become a gourmet cookie chef instead."

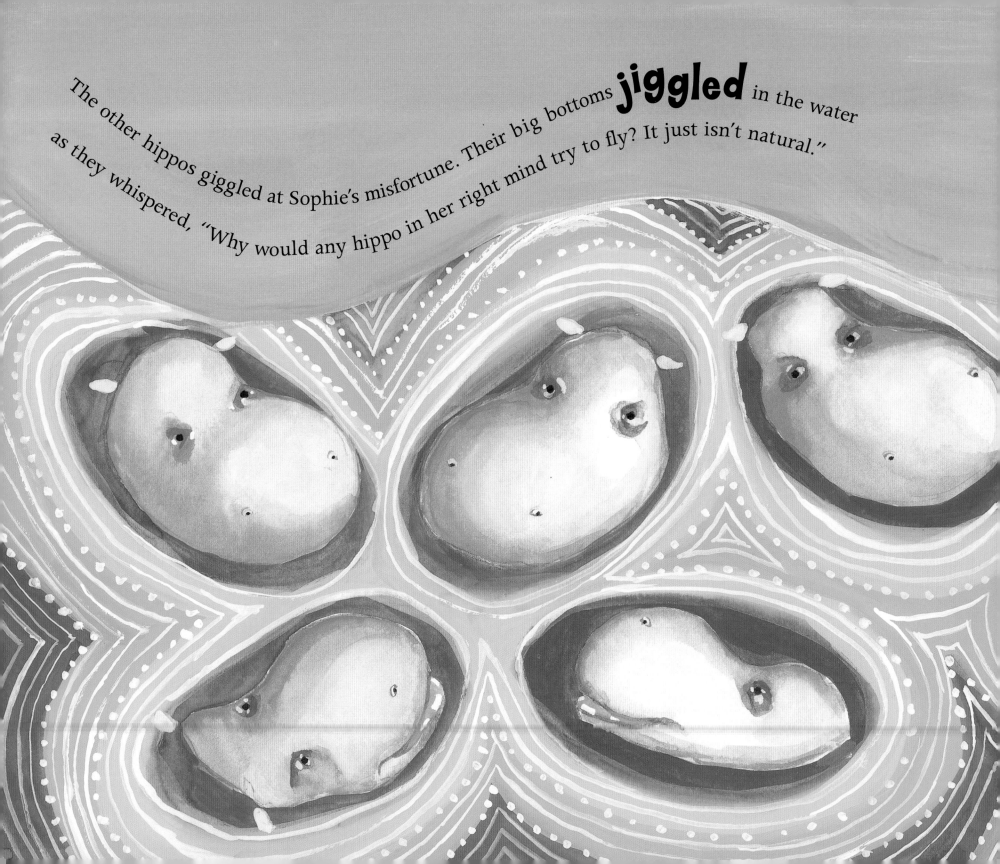

The other hippos giggled at Sophie's misfortune. Their big bottoms **jiggled** in the water as they whispered, "Why would any hippo in her right mind try to fly? It just isn't natural."

Still, they couldn't wait to see what Sophie would do next.

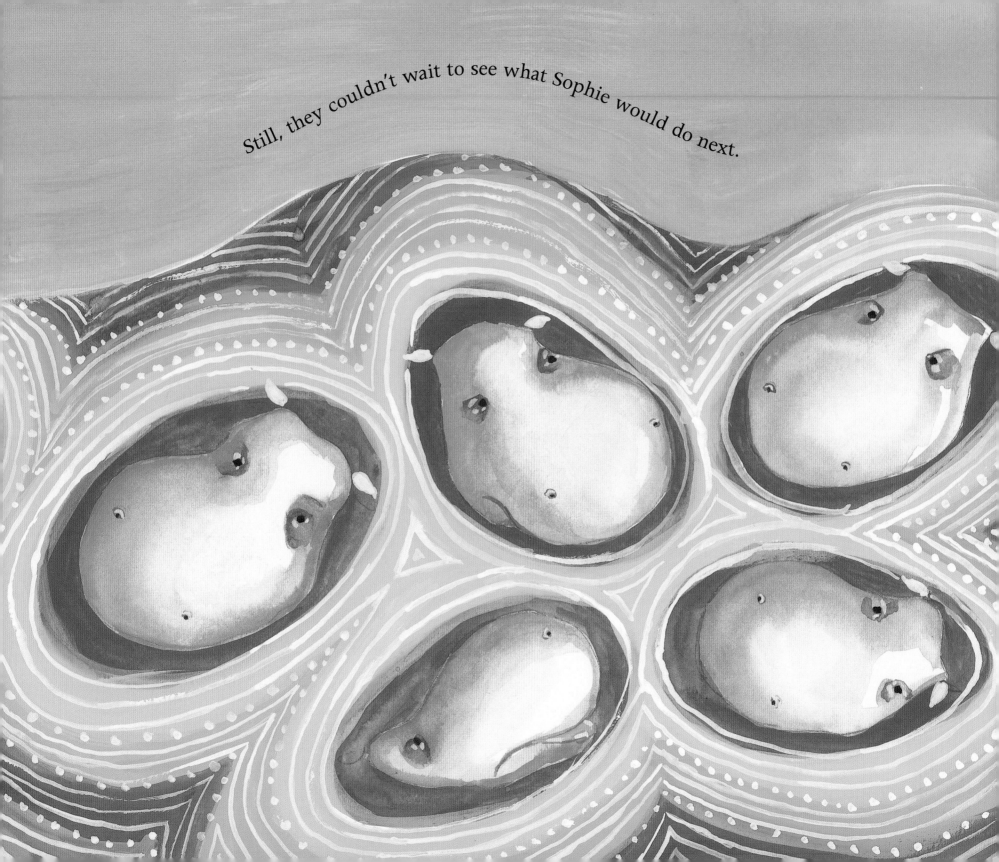

While Sophie spun her wheels on the ground, Sebastian tumbled out of his tree with a **THUD.** "I've got it!" he cried. "It's right here on page 568. To make your dream come true, you need inspiration. That means finding a new way to solve an old problem."

"Hmm," Sophie wondered. "Where will I find this inspiration?"

Taking a deep breath, she plunged to the bottom of the lake to think. Under the water it was cool and gloomy. Sophie blew some bubbles and got bored. But as she trudged back to shore, a tiny idea began to form in the back of her **GIGANTIC** head.

Excited by her inspiration, Sophie drew late into the night and didn't notice when Sebastian started to snore. She was *still* drawing when the sun came up the next morning.

At last Sophie shook Sebastian awake. "It's hot off the presses!" she announced. Sebastian pushed up his thick glasses and began to read.

It is a typical day in the life of Superhippo and Wonderbird.

Suddenly, they hear something . . .

When he was finished reading, Sebastian smiled. "You've finally done it, Sophie—you've made your dream come true!"

Whoosh! Before she could reply, a strong gust of wind blew Sebastian's glasses right off his beak. The wind blew everything off Sophie's drafting table, too.

"Oh, no!" she cried. "The ink isn't even dry yet!"

"This looks like a job for Wonderbird!" Sebastian shouted. But without his glasses, he zoomed off in the wrong direction.

Sophie watched as her precious comic sailed farther and farther away. Without a skateboard, she was too slow to save the day.

Meanwhile, the other hippos noticed that Sophie wasn't lounging on her favorite patch of grass. They blew **BIGGER** bubbles and gossiped about her more than ever.

After Sophie and Sebastian spent hours searching for the runaway comic,
they headed back to the lake.

"Look! It's Sophie!" cried one of the hippos.

All at once, twenty-four **BULGING** bodies crowded around her. "Do Superhippo and Wonderbird really save the day? Are there more adventures? What happens next?" they wanted to know.

Sophie thought for a moment, smiled, and then got back to work. When she was finished, Sebastian made twenty-four copies of her new comic masterpiece, **"THE UNSTOPPABLE DUO DOES IT AGAIN!"**

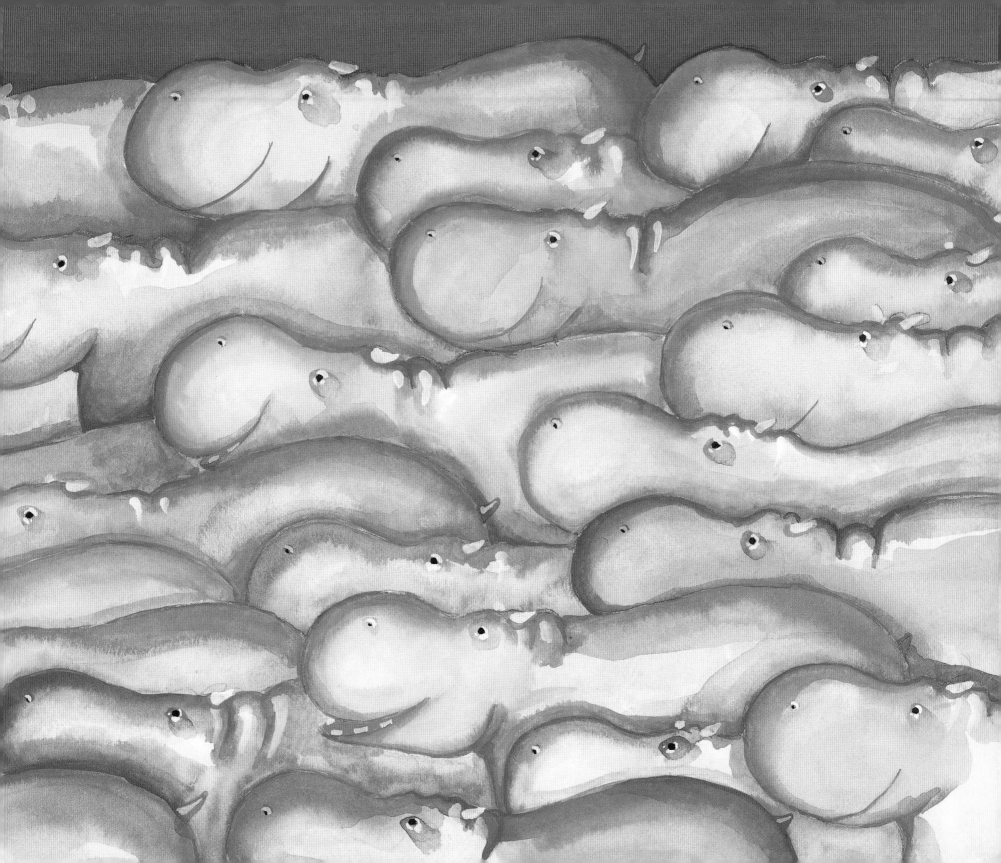

Important Words

continent one of Earth's seven main land areas.

global warming an increase in the average temperature of Earth's surface.

habitat a place where a living thing is naturally found.

mammal a member of a group of living beings. Mammals make milk to feed their babies and usually have hair or fur on their skin.

nutrient (NOO-tree-uhnt) something found in food that living beings take in to live and grow.

pollution human waste that dirties or harms air, water, or land.

prey an animal hunted or killed by a predator for food.

region a large part of the world that is different from other parts.

survive to continue to live or exist.

Web Sites

To learn more about polar bears, visit ABDO Publishing Company online. Web sites about polar bears are featured on our Book Links page. These links are routinely monitored and updated to provide the most current information available.

www.abdopublishing.com